-9. FEB. 1995		

L1066/4

L 1066

A STATE OF AFFAIRS

Stuttgart
Consequences
The Day of the Dog
Commitment

GRAHAM SWANNELL

faber and faber
LONDON · BOSTON

First published in 1985
by Faber and Faber Limited
3 Queen Square London WC1N 3AU

Photoset and printed in Great Britain by
Redwood Burn Ltd, Trowbridge, Wiltshire

British Library Cataloguing in Publication Data

Swannell, Graham
A state of affairs.
I. Title
822'.914   PR6069.W3/

ISBN 0–571–13858–6

To Harold Pinter
Thank You.

These plays were first performed at the Lyric Studio, Hammersmith, on 14 February 1985 with the following casts:

<table>
<tr><td></td><td>Stuttgart</td></tr>
<tr><td>TERENCE</td><td>Gary Bond</td></tr>
<tr><td>CAROLINE</td><td>Amanda Redman</td></tr>
</table>

<table>
<tr><td></td><td>Consequences</td></tr>
<tr><td>JACK</td><td>Gary Bond</td></tr>
<tr><td>FRANCES</td><td>Julie Legrand</td></tr>
<tr><td>MILLY</td><td>Amanda Redman</td></tr>
</table>

<table>
<tr><td></td><td>The Day of the Dog</td></tr>
<tr><td>ALLEN</td><td>Gary Bond</td></tr>
<tr><td>CLIFF</td><td>Peter Wight</td></tr>
<tr><td>MAURICE</td><td>Terence Hillyer</td></tr>
<tr><td>IRIS</td><td>Amanda Redman</td></tr>
<tr><td>VIRGINIA</td><td>Julie Legrand</td></tr>
</table>

<table>
<tr><td></td><td>Commitment</td></tr>
<tr><td>JOANNA</td><td>Amanda Redman</td></tr>
<tr><td>ELLIS</td><td>Gary Bond</td></tr>
<tr><td>JULIA</td><td>Julie Legrand</td></tr>
</table>

<table>
<tr><td>DIRECTOR</td><td>Peter James</td></tr>
<tr><td>SET DESIGNER</td><td>Tim Bickerton</td></tr>
<tr><td>COSTUMES</td><td>Brenda Murphy</td></tr>
<tr><td>LIGHTING</td><td>Dave Horn</td></tr>
</table>

They were subsequently produced at the Duchess Theatre, London, from 10 July 1985 with the following casts:

Stuttgart

TERENCE	Gary Bond
CAROLINE	Nichola McAuliffe

Consequences

JACK	Gary Bond
FRANCES	Amanda Boxer
MILLY	Nichola McAuliffe

The Day of the Dog

ALLEN	Gary Bond
CLIFF	Arthur Kelly
MAURICE	Lee Walker
TERRI	Nichola McAuliffe
VALERIE	Amanda Boxer

Commitment

JOANNA	Nichola McAuliffe
ELLIS	Gary Bond
JULIA	Amanda Boxer

DIRECTOR	Peter James
SET DESIGNER	Tim Bickerton
COSTUMES	Brenda Murphy
LIGHTING	Dave Horn

CONTENTS

STUTTGART

CHARACTERS

TERENCE	late thirties
CAROLINE	middle thirties

An expensively furnished bedroom in South-west London. Early evening.

TERENCE *stands in front of a mirror. He is dressed in a pair of blue underpants.*

TERENCE: (*Emphatically*) This has got to stop! I mean, look at you. You look absolutely shagged out. You can't go on like this any more. You have got to tell her. You have got to tell her the truth. Have I? Yes, I have. Right. (*Pause.*) Well, Caroline. . . I've been . . . thinking about what we do in bed. You know, 'The old bed business'. (*Pause.*) You see, It's about ducking into bed. Ducking under the covers and . . . doing it. Yes, doing it. Well, I really can't think of any other way of putting this, Caroline, except, do we have to? Do we really have to make love? So often?

I think she'll throw a fit if I say that.

Well, it's very difficult for me, Caroline, talking to you about sex because I know you like it. In fact you can't get enough of it. Whereas for me, personally speaking, I find it's beginning to pall. Pall? Yes, pall. Sex is beginning to pall.

Oh, no! No. It's me. It's not you. It's me. How could it be you? You are very beautiful. You have a wonderful body. Yes, you do. You know you do. Your body is extremely versatile. Extremely. (*Brief pause.*) It is, you know.

No. It's me. I must be getting long in the tooth. The magic's gone.

How can I put this? Having to do it when I don't particularly want to. Lying there waiting to begin. The same old motions. The same old grunts and groans. Well, it really is beginning to pall with me!

This isn't going to work, old son. This is not going to go down at all well. (*Brief pause.*) How can I put it?

Well, Caroline, my dear, I have actually been thinking about this for quite some time, and the point is, my sweet,

13

if we don't make love so often it doesn't mean I don't love you. Of course it doesn't. I love you, and love must be more than ducking into bed. Isn't it?

It's just you say, shall we do it? I think if I don't say, yes, you'll think I don't love you, and don't want you, and all that stuff. You know, all that stuff. So I blurt out, Yes! Let's do it! Even though I don't want to.

Mind you, I have to admit, in the past, once we'd got the old rhythm going, it could be all right, and sometimes it could be more than all right. In fact sometimes it could be bloody marvellous. Take Stuttgart. (*Brief pause.*) That was bloody marvellous, wasn't it? It was also a bloody long time ago.

No, these days, I can't get away from my first thought, when I hear you say with that particular look in your eye, when you say, Are you coming up, Terence? Well, my first thought is, Caroline, oh, Christ! Do we really have to?

I mean, I'm a regular fellow, but recently, well, it just doesn't excite me. God knows why.

I used to be, well, you know me. Anytime. Day or night. Anytime and more than once. Many times more than once. Even I amazed myself sometimes. I thought, you're bloody amazing you are. You even said I was amazing. With good reason. That was me. Anytime.

I don't know what's happened to me. I look at my watch and think, bloody hell, it's nearly ten-thirty! Bloody hell! I'll be at it within the hour. Or there I am sitting in my armchair, quietly reading in my armchair, when up you pop from behind the chair and start kissing me with your tongue. Well . . . your tongue. Actually there's nothing left to document about your tongue. I mean, there I am reading my Maupassant short stories when this 'Tongue' is thrust into my mouth. It is virtually down my throat. I'm on the point of choking I am. My head is crushed against the back of the chair and I'm suppose to cast aside my Maupassant and it's off with the old clothes and down on the carpet we go!

It's not as if we haven't done it before. It's not some new discovery. We have done it before. God knows how many times we've done it before. (*Brief pause.*) Well, it must be quite a few times. It's probably running into thousands of times. It's been what? Since . . . '69, well . . . that's quite a few thousand times isn't it? Well, actually it's bloody thousands of times! So it's safe to say, We know what it's like!

Somehow I've got off the point. What is the point?

The point is, Caroline, if we did it less, if we made love less, I think it might help me. I think it might help me regain my appetite.

How less?

Well, the figure that springs to mind. If we agreed to do it less. The figure that springs. Is . . . um . . . once a month. Yes. Once a month. What do you think?

She'll destroy me!

No, I think it's a very good idea, Caroline. I'm convinced, mind you, I've nothing to base this on, I'm quite prepared to concede I'm barking up the wrong tree, but I'm almost convinced that once a month sounds about right.

You see, if you had Dover Sole. Yes. Dover Sole. The fish. If you had Dover Sole every night of the week, and in the old days it was more than one Dover Sole a night. It was Dover Sole morning, noon and night. Well, if you had Dover Sole so often it stands to reason you'd pretty soon be sick to death of it. You'd scream, oh no, it's not Dover Sole again! Oh no, isn't there anything else? But. Dover Sole once a month. Well, that's a different story altogether. One could look forward to that. One might say, it's Dover Sole day tomorrow. That's something to look forward to. Also, and this is the other side of my point, I don't know about you, but to me a Dover Sole has a touch of quality about it. It certainly isn't something you throw down your throat in a hurry. A quick snack. No. You want to spend time over it. Gently ease it from its bones. Eat it with relish.

You've got my point, haven't you? You can see where this line of thinking leads. Excess. Devalues.

Still. Having said all that. I'm yours if you walk into the bedroom with nothing on but your boots. That kind of thing works. Correct me if I'm wrong, but I've never known it to fail. Well, it didn't fail in Stuttgart, did it? Mind you, what else can you do in Stuttgart? A rainy day in Stuttgart cries out for the old boots. I don't know what it is about those boots, you know, with the leather up the leg, not ankle boots, oh no, I'm not talking about ankle boots. I'm talking about leather ones with high heels and black silk stockings. Well, what can I say? Just the stockings, of course. I'm not talking about knickers. Good grief no! Well, did that work? That really worked. Still, how often does that happen now? Not often, and that's a fact.

Oh, this is no good! You've got to tell her. You've got to tell her the truth.

Well, Caroline, I went to see the doctor. I went to see Robert. He's just set up in Paradise Road. I said, Robert, the old bed business is getting to be a pain. The old instrument, you know, Rob, the old instrument, it's starting to fail me. Well, Terry, he said, it happens to all of us. It does, old man. We're friends, aren't we? We saw the Stones in Hyde Park. We go back. We even sat at the feet of Krishnamurti. My God, do we go back! And man to man, if you want my advice, have an affair.
(TERENCE *smiles*.)
What? I couldn't believe my ears. What you need is a bloody good affair. That'll get it working immediately. You see, Terry, you've been with Caroline since '69 and that's a hell of a long time. It's bound to go stale. I said, but Caroline is fantastic. Why should I go off her? Well, he said, we all know Caroline is gorgeous, Terry, but God knows why, it just, for absolutely no reason, it just packs up.

It was then I told him about my Dover Sole theory, Caroline, and, well, he just choked on his cigar. He said, don't be stupid, Terry. Don't try and be original. Just do what we all do and have a bloody fine affair. It's risky, but it's worth it.

(CAROLINE *enters*.)

CAROLINE: Aren't you ready yet?

TERENCE: Ah! Hello!

CAROLINE: Were you talking to yourself?

TERENCE: No.

CAROLINE: Well, hurry up. We're late.

TERENCE: Yes. Right.

(*Silence as* TERENCE *dresses and* CAROLINE *looks at herself in the mirror*.)

CAROLINE: Well, what do you think?

TERENCE: About what? (*Pause*.) What, darling? (*Pause*.) What!

CAROLINE: How do I look?

TERENCE: Oh, how do you look?

CAROLINE: Yes.

TERENCE: Well, you look, you know, you look all right.

CAROLINE: All right?

TERENCE: Yes, you look OK.

CAROLINE: OK? I look OK?

TERENCE: Yes.

CAROLINE: What are you talking about? I look terrific.

TERENCE: I'm sorry, Caroline.

CAROLINE: My God, I look bloody gorgeous! (*Pause*.) Well?

TERENCE: To tell you the truth, I feel a bit off colour.

CAROLINE: So what?

TERENCE: Well, I feel low.

CAROLINE: What's that got to do with it? I look bloody gorgeous. I want to hear you say it. Well?

TERENCE: You look bloody gorgeous.

CAROLINE: Thank you. (*Pause*.) What's the matter with you tonight? Eh?

TERENCE: Oh, you know how it is.

CAROLINE: How what is?

TERENCE: You know.

CAROLINE: What?

TERENCE: How it is when you get older. How things are.

CAROLINE: I'm not old. You speak for yourself. How dare you say I'm old.

TERENCE: You are thirty-five, you know.

CAROLINE: So?

TERENCE: So.

CAROLINE: What are you trying to say?

TERENCE: Nothing.

CAROLINE: (*After a brief pause.*) If anyone's old it's you. You're nearly forty.

TERENCE: I know.

CAROLINE: Forty!

TERENCE: All right.

CAROLINE: You're almost fifty!

TERENCE: All right. All right! I told you I was getting old. That's how it is. You get old and things start to happen. (*Pause.*)

CAROLINE: I don't look thirty-five. Well . . . Do I?

TERENCE: No, you don't look thirty-five.

CAROLINE: Really?

TERENCE: No, you look bloody gorgeous you do.

CAROLINE: You're just saying that.

TERENCE: No, I'm not.

CAROLINE: Well, if I don't look thirty-five how old do I look?

TERENCE: (*After a pause.*) Twenty-seven?

CAROLINE: Twenty-seven?

TERENCE: Twenty-six.

CAROLINE: Twenty-six. Really? Really?

TERENCE: Yes.

CAROLINE: Oh, good. Good. I'm glad I've still got it. It makes me feel good. I feel good tonight. I feel up for it.

(CAROLINE *embraces* TERENCE.)

You know, I'm probably in my prime. Do you think I'm in my prime? Terence? You should be glad your old lady is in her prime.

TERENCE: I think I ought to talk to you.

CAROLINE: Talk?

TERENCE: Yes. Talk.

CAROLINE: We're going out, Terry. We're late already. There's no time to talk. You know what Dick and Alice are like. You know what that Barnes lot are like.

TERENCE: I have to talk to you.

CAROLINE: What? Talk talk?

TERENCE: Yes.

CAROLINE: What about?

TERENCE: Well. I . . .
    (*Pause.*)

CAROLINE: Oh, my God.

TERENCE: What?

CAROLINE: I don't believe it.

TERENCE: What? What!

CAROLINE: You're not, are you? You're not having a . . .

TERENCE: What!

CAROLINE: An affair.

TERENCE: Oh, no! No! Oh, good God, no! (*Brief pause.*) No. No.
    (*Pause.*)

CAROLINE: No?

TERENCE: No.
    (*Pause.*)

CAROLINE: Are you sure?

TERENCE: Of course I'm sure. I'd know if I was. (*Brief pause.*) I mean, I'd know.

CAROLINE: Well, thank God for that.

TERENCE: Yes.

CAROLINE: So what's so important?

TERENCE: Well . . . I went to see Robert.

CAROLINE: Is something wrong with you?

TERENCE: I'm a bit off colour. I told you.

CAROLINE: I'm sorry, darling, I didn't believe you. What did he say?

TERENCE: Oh, it's nothing. Nothing. We can talk about all this when we get back.

CAROLINE: No, I want to know. What's the matter? Are you ill?

TERENCE: (*After a pause.*) I really don't know how to tell you.

CAROLINE: Terry?
(CAROLINE *sits*.)
What is it, Terry?
TERENCE: Oh, hell. (*Brief pause*.) Well, the truth is, Caroline, I think I've gone off you.
(*Pause*.)
CAROLINE: Gone off me?
TERENCE: Yes.
(*Pause*.)
CAROLINE: Me?
TERENCE: Yes.
CAROLINE: How can you go off me? I'm bloody gorgeous.
TERENCE: Yes. Well, Robert said. . .
CAROLINE: What?
TERENCE: Robert said . . .
CAROLINE: You've talked about this with Robert?
TERENCE: Well, yes.
CAROLINE: You've talked to that weekend hippie about me?
TERENCE: Yes.
(*Pause*.)
CAROLINE: Well? What did he have to say for himself?
TERENCE: Oh, Christ. You'll never believe this, Caroline, but Robert actually advised me to have an affair.
CAROLINE: What?
TERENCE: I know.
CAROLINE: He told you to have an affair?
TERENCE: I know. I can't think what possessed him. (*Pause*.) Except he did say, it does go off for most couples. It's quite normal for most couples to go off each other. That's why I'm not up for it. That's why I'm off it. And the pressure, of course. The pressure to keep on making love.
CAROLINE: You little creep!
TERENCE: Creep?
CAROLINE: You're having a bloody affair!
TERENCE: I'm not!
CAROLINE: Who is she? Do I know her?

TERENCE: Oh, come on, Caroline, give us a chance. I only talked to Robert last week.

CAROLINE: You mean to say you've had a whole week and you haven't managed to pull anyone?

TERENCE: Of course not.

CAROLINE: Why? What's the matter with you? Don't tell me you've lost the old chat. The charm. (*Pause*.) I don't believe it. Have an affair! Christ!

TERENCE: Yes. I know. (*Pause*.) Well, what do you think? Do you think I should?

CAROLINE: Are you serious?

TERENCE: No. No. It's a joke!

CAROLINE: You are serious.

TERENCE: No, I'm not! (*Brief pause*.) Mind you, if you think I should. If you think it might help us. I suppose, for you, I could face it. I could force myself. I suppose. For you. I could force myself. (*Pause*.) Caroline?

CAROLINE: Let me get this straight. You say, you've gone off it with me.

TERENCE: Yes.

CAROLINE: What about me?

TERENCE: You? Oh, you love it. You can't get enough of it.

CAROLINE: Yes. I like married sex. It's just sex, isn't it? There's no pretence about liking each other. We both know what we want and we don't have to give out a lot of chat to get it. It's just good hard sex.

TERENCE: Is it?

CAROLINE: However. Since it's the 'Old Truth Time'.

TERENCE: The what?

CAROLINE: The reason I do it with you so often. The reason it happens so often. It's because I think you want it.

TERENCE: Me? Want it?

CAROLINE: I think, Oh, I better do it. Sometimes I'd rather have a cup of cocoa and read my book, but I think, Oh, I better do it, otherwise he'll start to whinge.

TERENCE: Whinge?

CAROLINE: I can't bear it when you whinge.

TERENCE: I don't whinge.

CAROLINE: Yes, you do.

TERENCE: I don't whinge! When do I whinge? Are you telling me you only make love to stop me whingeing?

CAROLINE: Sometimes.

TERENCE: (*After a brief pause.*) I don't believe it.

CAROLINE: Of course there are other times.

TERENCE: Other times? You mean, most of the time?

CAROLINE: No, just sometimes, when I like a good session. Of course, more often than not, it's not a good session.

TERENCE: It's not?

CAROLINE: No.

TERENCE: Really?

CAROLINE: Yes... It's pretty bad sometimes.

TERENCE: Bad?

CAROLINE: Yes, it's pretty bad.

TERENCE: I always thought it was rather good.

CAROLINE: You would.

(*Pause.*)

TERENCE: Oh, come on, sometimes it's been good.

CAROLINE: You only remember the good ones. The good sessions. Like Stuttgart.

TERENCE: Stuttgart? Oh yes, Stuttgart was good.

CAROLINE: Yes, it was good. It really was quite good.

TERENCE: Actually it was bloody marvellous.

CAROLINE: Mmmnn.

TERENCE: Bloody marvellous.

(*Pause.*)

CAROLINE: Well, it's obvious what you need.

TERENCE: What?

CAROLINE: You need another Stuttgart.

TERENCE: I'm not capable of another Stuttgart!

CAROLINE: I am.

TERENCE: Well, we all know you are.

CAROLINE: So are you.

TERENCE: No, I don't think so. I mean, Stuttgart was pretty acrobatic.

CAROLINE: Yes, it was virtually airborne.
(*Pause.*)

TERENCE: Are you seriously telling me we've been ducking under the covers when neither of us really wanted to?

CAROLINE: Mmmnn.

TERENCE: You haven't been doing it out of pity? (*Brief pause.*) Have you?

CAROLINE: (*After reflection.*) No.

TERENCE: Are you sure?

CAROLINE: Oh, sometimes it's all right, Terry. It can be quite pleasant really. Sometimes.

TERENCE: Really?

CAROLINE: Yes, but it's got nothing to do with you.

TERENCE: What!

CAROLINE: No, it's all to do with me. It just depends on whether I feel up for it. If I am, I know how to get you going.

TERENCE: Get me going?

CAROLINE: Yes.

TERENCE: Well, it all sounds a bloody effort to me!

CAROLINE: No, it's no effort.
(*Pause.*)

TERENCE: Christ! Let me get this straight before I do something really stupid. Are you telling me that I . . . that I . . . don't turn you on any more? Caroline? (*Pause.*) I don't believe it. Caroline? What's wrong with me?

CAROLINE: Sometimes you turn me on, dear.

TERENCE: I do?

CAROLINE: Mmmnn.

TERENCE: When?

CAROLINE: Oh, you know.

TERENCE: No, I don't. You tell me.

CAROLINE: Ah, let's see. Well . . . I like it when you're walking on a beach and I see other women fancy you. That turns me on.

TERENCE: Is that all! What about my body? Doesn't my body do anything for you?

CAROLINE: Well, I suppose it's all right.

TERENCE: All right!

CAROLINE: Yes, it's all right.

TERENCE: All right! After all these years, all these bloody years, and it's only all right?

CAROLINE: It's OK, Terry, I've settled for it.

TERENCE: What did you say?

CAROLINE: I've settled for it.

TERENCE: Settled for it!

CAROLINE: I know there's probably better out there, you know, better bodies . . .

TERENCE: Better bodies?

CAROLINE: Yes, but I think, what's the point? I can't be bothered with all that. No, I'll settle for this. Anyway I have settled for it.

TERENCE: I'm not something you settle for. God damn it, I'm not that!

CAROLINE: But I'm prepared to accept it. That is enough for me. I know there is probably better but I accept it.

TERENCE: I thought you loved me.

CAROLINE: I do. I love you. I care for you.

TERENCE: How can you, if you've only settled for me?

CAROLINE: (*Tenderly*) But, Terry, I picked you. I picked you out.

TERENCE: Picked me out?

CAROLINE: Of course.

TERENCE: Bloody picked me out?

CAROLINE: Yes.

TERENCE: I thought I swept you off your feet. Didn't I? (*Pause.*) I had a feeling bringing all this up was a bad idea. Idiot!

CAROLINE: What did you expect, Terence? You stand there with a schoolboy grin on your face and tell me the doctor thinks you should have an affair. I wasn't born yesterday. (*Silence.*)

TERENCE: When we were at it in Stuttgart, that was real, wasn't it? You weren't just doing it for me?

CAROLINE: Of course not. Mind you, those mirrors helped. I'll never forget those mirrors.

TERENCE: All right! All right! Having an affair was Robert's idea not mine. It wasn't, you know. I had a completely different idea.

CAROLINE: What? That I should have the affair?

TERENCE: Good God, no!

(*Pause.*)

CAROLINE: Well?

TERENCE: If we don't make love so often it doesn't mean I don't love you.

CAROLINE: Doesn't it?

TERENCE: Of course it doesn't. I love you and love must be more than ducking into bed. Isn't it?

CAROLINE: Well...

TERENCE: Oh, come on, Caroline! Give us a break!

CAROLINE: Well, it certainly helps. Doing it, helps.

TERENCE: But if we did it less. If we agreed to do it less.

CAROLINE: What do you mean? Like what? Every few days?

TERENCE: Well ... no ...

CAROLINE: Once a week?

TERENCE: Well ... no ... no ...

CAROLINE: Are you serious? Once a fortnight?

TERENCE: Well, no, I was thinking more in terms of once a month.

CAROLINE: Once a month! Once a bloody month!

TERENCE: I knew you'd throw a fit.

CAROLINE: This is not a fit.

TERENCE: It looks like a fit.

CAROLINE: Once a month! What bloody book have you been reading?

TERENCE: No, listen! Listen to me.

CAROLINE: What?

TERENCE: It's like Dover Sole.

CAROLINE: Dover Sole?

TERENCE: Yes. Dover Sole. The fish. You don't want Dover Sole every meal.

CAROLINE: What are you talking about? You know I hate fish.

TERENCE: Ah! Damn! Still, if we did it less . . .

CAROLINE: Oh, do shut up, Terence!

TERENCE: Well, I'm sure we're not supposed to do it so often! Hammering away night after night! I can't keep it going any more! I'm not just here for your pleasure!

CAROLINE: Aren't you?

TERENCE: Of course I'm not!

CAROLINE: You really do need a session.

TERENCE: What?

CAROLINE: You need a lively session and you need it now!

TERENCE: Now?

CAROLINE: Right now.

TERENCE: Oh, no!

CAROLINE: Oh, yes!

(TERENCE *starts to put on his shoes.*)

TERENCE: I thought we were going out?

CAROLINE: They can wait.

(CAROLINE *struggles with* TERENCE *over his shoes.*)

TERENCE: Get off! I don't want to do it now.

CAROLINE: I do.

(*Off come* TERENCE's *shoes.*)

I fancy another Stuttgart.

TERENCE: Another Stuttgart?

CAROLINE: That should do the trick.

TERENCE: Another Stuttgart? Now!

(CAROLINE *gets a pair of black boots out of the wardrobe.*)

Oh, bloody hell!

CAROLINE: What do you think? The old boots, eh?

TERENCE: Oh, bloody hell. (*Pause.*) Is this what it's come to? Is this what it has finally come to?

CAROLINE: But it's nice, Terry. It's extremely nice.

TERENCE: You're going to wipe me out, Caroline. You might even kill me!

CAROLINE: I can't think of a better way to go.

TERENCE: I tell you, being a man these days is not much fun. It's beginning to be bloody awful. I don't want to do it!

CAROLINE: Relax, Terence.

TERENCE: Why does it have to be me? Why do I have to perform all the time? Why has it got to be me hammering away all the time?

(CAROLINE *steps out of her dress. She wears black underwear.*)

Oh, my God!

(*Pause.*)

CAROLINE: It's all right, Terry. You don't have to do anything.

TERENCE: What?

CAROLINE: You don't have to do anything.

TERENCE: What do you mean?

CAROLINE: All I want you to do is lie on the bed.

TERENCE: I beg your pardon?

CAROLINE: All you have to do is lie there.

(*Pause.*)

TERENCE: Lie here?

CAROLINE: Yes. I'll do it all. You don't have to perform. You just have to lie there. On your back.

(*Pause.*)

TERENCE: Really?

CAROLINE: Yes. All you have to do is be here. As long as you're not elsewhere everything will be just fine. As long as you're not elsewhere.

(*Pause.*)

TERENCE: I wasn't really thinking of going elsewhere. I wasn't, you know.

CAROLINE: Weren't you?

TERENCE: Would I lie?

(CAROLINE *pulls on the boots. Pause.*)

CAROLINE: I think you ought to take your clothes off.

TERENCE: (*After a pause.*) Mmm.

(TERENCE *undresses and stands there in his underpants.*) I feel shy. I feel as if I don't know you. (*Pause.*) All I have to do is lie here? On my back?

CAROLINE: Yes.

TERENCE: Well, if that's what you want.

27

CAROLINE: Do I have a choice?

TERENCE: Actually I'm quite good at lying on my back. (*Pause.* TERENCE *lies on the bed.*)

CAROLINE: Comfortable?

TERENCE: Yes, thank you. (*Pause.*) Well? What are you waiting for? (*Pause.*) Caroline? (*Pause.*) Eh?

CAROLINE: The lights.

BLACKOUT

CONSEQUENCES

CHARACTERS

JACK	forties
FRANCES	middle thirties
MILLY	middle thirties

A cheap and sparsely furnished hotel room in West London. Mid winter. Late afternoon.

Cold light.
Two beds, one soiled.
JACK *and* FRANCES *in their underwear. They dress in silence.*

JACK: Christ, this lino's cold! You'd think with all the money they've had off us they could at least afford a scrap of carpet. (*Pause.*) I bet the traffic's building up over Kew Bridge.

FRANCES: Finish me off, will you?
(JACK *zips her up. They embrace. Silence.*)

JACK: You didn't happen to notice where I put my socks?

FRANCES: I wasn't looking at your socks.

JACK: Weren't you? (*Brief pause.*) Well ... you can be sure Milly will notice I've no socks. She's bound to notice when I undress.

FRANCES: You undress in front of each other?

JACK: Don't you?
(FRANCES *makes up.*)

FRANCES: I haven't stripped off in front of Michael for ages, and I can't remember the last time I saw him naked.

JACK: (*Laughs.*) Michael naked.

FRANCES: Yes, he moved his clothes into the spare room when he started to put on weight. He didn't want me to see his stomach. Mind you, I didn't want to see it either. Who wants to see a large expanse of white flesh the last thing at night? Cigarette?

JACK: I must find these socks.
(JACK *looks under the bed.* FRANCES *lights a cigarette.*)

JACK: Dear God, the filth under here. Ah!

FRANCES: Success?

JACK: How the hell did they get under here?
(JACK *emerges with his socks.*) I must have kicked them under there in the rush.

FRANCES: Mmmnn.
(*Silence.* JACK *puts on his socks and shoes.*)

JACK: Well . . . that's that. Ready yet?

FRANCES: Nearly.

JACK: Good. (*Pause.*) I must say it was very pleasant today. A very pleasant afternoon. Don't you agree?

FRANCES: Of course. It was extremely pleasant.

JACK: Yes, wasn't it?

FRANCES: It was probably one of our best.

JACK: If not the best.

FRANCES: Yes, possibly the best. (*Brief pause.*) You're very good, you know.

JACK: Well. You're quite good too.

FRANCES: Were you taught?

JACK: What?

FRANCES: Were you shown the ropes? Did some older woman show you the ropes?

JACK: Oh, no. I never had that kind of luck! No, I had to pick it up as I went along. The great thing is to keep at it.

FRANCES: Of course.

(*Pause.*)

JACK: I think I will have that cigarette. I fancy a smoke before we belt off home.

(JACK *takes a cigarette.* FRANCES *embraces him.*)

Oh, I say . . .

(*She kisses him.*)

Do you think it's wise if we start up again?

(*A passionate kiss.*)

We're dressed, Frances. It's such a bore to take off all the clobber.

FRANCES: It's only a kiss.

JACK: Ah, yes. I keep forgetting. A kiss with Milly means all the way. I was responding out of habit.

(*Pause.* FRANCES *touches up her lips.* JACK *lights his cigarette.*)

FRANCES: Well? Will I do?

JACK: Oh, I should say so. If I saw you on the other side of the street I'd certainly cross over for a closer inspection.

(JACK *prepares to leave.*)

FRANCES: Do you do that often?

32

JACK: Well . . .

FRANCES: How often?

JACK: Oh, you know blokes.

FRANCES: No. I don't know.

JACK: Hey, don't spoil it, Frances. I'm enjoying this cigarette. I haven't enjoyed a cigarette like this for ages. OK?

FRANCES: (*After a brief pause.*) It's awfully grim here.

JACK: What?

FRANCES: This is a depressing little hole.

JACK: Is it?

FRANCES: Why do we have to meet in such a grim place?

JACK: Oh, that's a searching question.

FRANCES: Why does it have to be so grim?

JACK: Well . . . I suppose we could splash out next time.

FRANCES: Splash out?

JACK: Yes, you know, I think it's treats time, next time. A place with carpet, and afterwards tea and hot buttered toast.

FRANCES: I'd want champagne.

JACK: Champagne? Oh, yes. Excellent. Champagne before, tea afterwards. It's always good, the odd glass of champagne. It tends to thaw the ice.

FRANCES: I wasn't aware of any ice.

JACK: Ah, well, you know, one minute you're squashed in the traffic. The next you're squashed between the sheets. It's a bit drastic, isn't it? No, champagne would ease the passage. Smooth one out for the sheets. Set one up, so to speak. (*Pause.*) Don't you agree, Frances?

FRANCES: What? Oh, yes, I enjoy it with champagne.

JACK: Well, that's what we'll do! (*Pause.*) Of course, if you want a real change, what would be really splendid would be a large room with a bay window overlooking the sea. We could sit by the bay window watching the sea. There'd be sunlight through the net curtains. We'd sip our champagne.

FRANCES: It's winter. There wouldn't be sunlight. There'd be drizzle. Grey drizzle. Grey sea.

JACK: No! You always get sunlight in winter.

FRANCES: When?

JACK: When? All the time. We've all seen sunlight in winter.
(JACK *checks his watch.*)
Oh, yes, I can see it now. Sunlight on the bed and warm
too. Big warm radiators. Not like this pit!
(JACK *sits close to* FRANCES.)
You see, that's the trouble with winter. It does tend to get a
bit chilly, and that does tend to hamper the process. One is
reluctant to take off one's woolly. I mean, it's not quite the
same with your woolly on, is it? Somehow you don't get the
same charge. That touch of skin on skin. Of course yours is
a nice enough woolly, as woollies go, but frankly it's what's
underneath that I come here for.

FRANCES: (*After a pause.*) Jack.

JACK: What?

FRANCES: Can I ask you a question?

JACK: Oh hello.

FRANCES: I really would appreciate an honest answer.

JACK: Well, you know me. I'm a fairly honest fellow. One does
one's best.

FRANCES: Do you love me? (*Pause.*) Jack?

JACK: Is that it? Is that the question?

FRANCES: Yes.

JACK: Do I love you?

FRANCES: It's not a difficult question.

JACK: (*After a brief pause.*) Well, to be perfectly frank. If you
want it straight from the shoulder. My answer would have
to be no.
(*Pause.*)

FRANCES: No?

JACK: No, I don't love you. I'm sorry. You wanted me to be
honest. There it is I'm afraid.

FRANCES: You don't love me?

JACK: No.

FRANCES: Have you ever loved me?

JACK: Well, how can I put this without . . .

FRANCES: You've never loved me?

JACK: This is awfully depressing, Frances! Can't we talk about something else?

FRANCES: That time when we met at Waterloo and walked across Hungerford Bridge. You didn't love me that time?

JACK: What? Where?

FRANCES: When we sat by the river in the sun. You didn't love me?

JACK: Oh, Christ, look at the time!

FRANCES: I don't believe you.

JACK: This will have to wait, Frances. It nearly slipped my mind. Milly's got her cousins round this evening. I'm supposed to be there listening to their stories and pouring drink down their throats. Hell! I've got to go. I know it seems like I'm doing a bunk, but honestly I've got to dash. You've had to dash before, haven't you? You've often had to dash before! Look, look, I'll tell you what . . . we'll talk about all this the next time. OK? (*Kisses* FRANCES.) I'll give you a ring. OK? Till the next time. I really must dash. (*Exit* JACK. *Silence.* FRANCES *puts her make-up into her handbag. Pause. She stands up and slowly puts on her coat. Pause.*)

FRANCES: (*Screams.*) Arrgh!
(*She wrecks the beds. Pause.* JACK *rushes back.*)

JACK: What the hell's going on, Frances? There's people out in the corridor.
(*Pause.* FRANCES *stands amid the wrecked beds.*)
I thought you were upset. I was going to come back anyway. I thought, what am I? Am I a complete arsehole? (*Brief pause.*) The cousins can pour their own drinks. I'll lie. I've lied before. It'll just be another lie to go with all the other lies. (*Pause.*) I'm back, Frances. I know I didn't get very far, but anyway, I'm back. (*Pause.*) Oh, no.

FRANCES: What?

JACK: You can't be.

FRANCES: What is it, Jack?

JACK: (*Wearily*) You're not in love with me, are you?

FRANCES: Mmm.

35

JACK: Oh, no. Are you sure?

FRANCES: Yes.

JACK: Oh, come on, Frances. How can you love me?

FRANCES: It's quite easy to love you.

JACK: But I'm worthless. I'm practically a slob. You can't love a worthless slob. (*Brief pause.*) This is bloody awful. You've broken the rules.

FRANCES: What rules?

JACK: From the first day. We decided. We agreed. That it would be foolish. No, worse than foolish, that it would be a bloody cock-up if we fell in love. We agreed. I fancied you. You fancied me. That was it. We even shook hands on it. We laughed ourselves sick. Fall in love, we said. You must be joking!

FRANCES: I've loved you ever since the four of us took our kids to that bowling alley.

JACK: (*After a pause.*) Bowling alley?

FRANCES: You were wearing jeans that day.

JACK: Jeans?

FRANCES: It was probably the way you bent over to pick up your bowl.

JACK: Oh, Frances, that's not love. That's lust.

FRANCES: No, it's not. (*Pause.*) Then Milly came and sat on your knee and I got all steamed up and had to go and stand in a telephone booth until I'd cooled off.

JACK: Oh, yes! I remember you in the telephone booth. You know, Milly said you were probably calling your lover. (*Pause.*)

FRANCES: I've never had a lover till you.

JACK: Oh, come on, I'm not your lover.

FRANCES: Aren't you? Don't you call all this being lovers? Has this got nothing to do with love?

JACK: Christ, don't say that, Frances. You're making me sweat. Look.

FRANCES: I think about you all the time.

JACK: Well, I think about you.

FRANCES: Do you? Really?

36

JACK: Yes, of course I do. I often catch myself thinking about you.

FRANCES: What do you think?

JACK: Oh, I don't know. I just think about you.

FRANCES: You must remember what you think.

JACK: Oh, you know. Thoughts! How do you think I feel? (*Pause*.) Christ, Frances, you're making this very difficult for me!

FRANCES: I didn't mean to make it difficult.

JACK: Well, it's not my fault. I'm not to blame. I kept my side of the contract. It's not my fault you've fallen for me.

FRANCES: No.

JACK: I mean, I can't stop women falling for me.

FRANCES: That's true. But it might help if you didn't get into their beds.

JACK: Oh, listen, I don't do this with every woman I know.

FRANCES: Really? There's no one else?

JACK: I have a wife. I already see you. It leaves me very little time for anyone else.

FRANCES: But if you had time?

JACK: Well, you know . . .

FRANCES: My God.

JACK: What does that mean? My God? What's that supposed to mean? (*Pause*.)

FRANCES: I can't bear the thought of you with another woman. I especially can't bear the thought of you with your wife. Dear Milly. I want to cut her throat.

JACK: What?

FRANCES: I hate her.

JACK: You hate Milly?

FRANCES: Passionately.

JACK: Why? Milly hasn't harmed you.

FRANCES: She exists, doesn't she?

JACK: (*After a pause.*) Oh, come on, Milly's all right.

FRANCES: I want to be with you all the time. I want to wake up with you.

JACK: Wake up with me? Have you any idea what I'm like in the morning?

FRANCES: I want to wake up with you in a clean room. Between clean sheets. I want to wake up as your wife.

JACK: As what?

FRANCES: I want to be married to you.

(*Pause.*)

JACK: Marriage.

FRANCES: Mmmnn.

JACK: Good grief. (*Silence.*) Well ... Well... What can I say? It's obvious all this has got to stop.

FRANCES: Stop?

JACK: There's no point. We mustn't see each other again.

FRANCES: Mustn't see each other?

JACK: This is absolutely terrible. Marry you?

FRANCES: Why not?

JACK: What's the point? We're both married already!

FRANCES: I love you.

JACK: But what about Michael?

FRANCES: Michael? Michael hasn't laid a finger on me for years.

JACK: (*After a pause.*) He hasn't?

FRANCES: No. Not a finger.

JACK: Oh, my God.

(*Pause.*)

FRANCES: If anyone's a slob it's Michael. He's not the man I married. I married a rather trim man with hair on his head. Since the first day he's let himself go. He got me and that was that. He doesn't care what I think. He comes into the room and I can smell his feet before he takes off his shoes.

JACK: What? They can't be that bad.

FRANCES: They stink.

JACK: Well, it's a common enough affliction, Frances.

FRANCES: One of the first reasons I liked you was because you washed.

JACK: What was that?

FRANCES: I'll tell you what broke my back. It was the evening paper.

JACK: The *Standard*?

FRANCES: The newsagent's only round the corner. It shouldn't take him five minutes to get a paper, but he's never back within the hour.

JACK: Ah.

FRANCES: You know where he is, don't you?

JACK: Well. What's wrong with a pint?

FRANCES: Pint? Pints! He comes back stinking of beer and then he has the nerve to say, they'd sold out round the corner, Fanny. I had to nip down to the station to get one. I say to him, why don't you place an order round the corner? That way you won't have to walk to the station every night. He says, oh no, I can't be bothered with orders. Except I checked. He does have an order. He never goes to the station. He just dives into the pub and chats about sport to the landlord. I know this because I met the landlord's wife, and she told me how her husband and Michael are always nattering on about cricket or rugby.

JACK: It must have been a blow when the *Saturday Evening News* packed up.

FRANCES: Sunday's worse. He's very nervy on Sunday.

JACK: Who isn't? Sometimes I feel seven o'clock will never come.

FRANCES: (*After a pause.*) It's the fact he has to lie to me over such a trivial matter. It makes me feel as if I'm his mother not his wife.

(FRANCES *weeps silently.*)

JACK: Well, you lie about us. I lie to Milly. We lie every day. Every hour probably. To ourselves. To our friends. I mean, we're lying all over the place. (*Pause.*) You just can't condemn a man over a pint. That's not fair. A pint's a pint. I have a pint. Michael has a pint. I've frequently bought him pints and he's bought me pints. We even shared pints in the old days, and talked about rugby. We frequently talk about rugby. We usually end up talking about Richard Sharpe's hands. You wouldn't know about Richard Sharpe, but his hands! The way he ran with the ball. One hand wrapped round it. We haven't seen his like since . . .

FRANCES: (*Fiercely*) Rugby is a game for mental defectives!

JACK: Hey, steady on old girl.

FRANCES: I've told him anyway.

JACK: Told who what?

FRANCES: There is no lie. I've told Michael.

JACK: (*Pausing*) You can't have.

FRANCES: I have.

JACK: You've told Michael about us?

FRANCES: I told him this morning.

JACK: You're kidding me. Aren't you? (*Pause.*) You've told him?

FRANCES: Mmmnn.

JACK: Christ! Mick knows? What the hell did he say?

FRANCES: He said, he always knew you were a bastard.

JACK: What! This is bloody appalling! You told Mick we've been having a ding dong?

FRANCES: A ding dong!

JACK: Why? Why tell him when it's only a ding dong! How can you? I'm absolutely appalled!
(*Pause.*)

FRANCES: Well, there's worse to come.

JACK: Worse?

FRANCES: Mmm.

JACK: What could be worse than this for Christ's sake?

FRANCES: Milly knowing.

JACK: No!

FRANCES: Yes, I think so.

JACK: What do you mean, you think so? Does she or doesn't she?

FRANCES: I think Michael's gone to see her.

JACK: Oh, no! How could he? You're bloody mad! You stupid bitch!

FRANCES: Jack!

JACK: You've ruined everything!

FRANCES: But I love you.

JACK: Love! Love! I've had enough of love. I'm sick to death of

40

love! Why can't you all leave me alone? You. Milly. My mother. You're all at it!

FRANCES: But Jack, I can't live like this any longer.

JACK: Love! I'm not cut out for it. I haven't got what it takes! All right, all right, you can have it straight. I just like getting between the sheets. That's what I like. What do you think I am? I like getting between the sheets as much as the next person, but that's it. That's as far as it goes. I mean, what do you want? You want lies? You want promises? Is that what you want? Why didn't you talk to me first? Why didn't you check with me? How the hell am I going to face Milly!

(*Pause.*)

FRANCES: I really thought you loved me.

JACK: We were going along very nicely, Frances! We were having a nice time!

FRANCES: I want more.

JACK: More?

FRANCES: Yes.

JACK: More of what?

FRANCES: More of you!

JACK: Me? There is no more of me! This is it. This is all there is, Frances.

FRANCES: I can't live any longer not knowing when I'll see you next. I want to stay together. Plan the future . . . children . . .

JACK: More kids? More kids! You've got kids, I've got kids! We know what kids are. Christ! You've got a bloody screw loose!

FRANCES: Oh yes! I see. I see. It's all right for you. This is just what you want. It's so very cosy without the responsibilities.

JACK: I've got enough responsibilities at home. Who needs a double dose?

FRANCES: OK! OK! I've got your point. By God, have I got your point!

JACK: No! You haven't got the point! I mean, somedays I look at you and I feel good, other days it's as if I'm in another country. That's how I feel. I mean, I could say the words, I love you, but what does it mean? Have you ever thought about it?

FRANCES: It's not something you think about, it's something you feel.

JACK: Oh yes? What does it feel like?

FRANCES: You don't know? You really don't know?

JACK: Listen, I could hand you all kinds of garbage. All kinds of crap. But really if it's the truth, if it's the truth you really want, I have to say, I don't think I've ever loved. Unless you're talking about what I feel for the kids. But that's blood. I'd kill for them!

FRANCES: I'm so angry! So angry!

JACK: Frances, be quiet! People will hear you!

FRANCES: I don't care. Let them hear. I'm so angry! How can you discuss love so coldly? Discuss us so coldly? It makes me want to scream!
(*She screams.*)

JACK: Frances, shut up. Shut up!
(JACK *attempts to quieten* FRANCES *by putting his hand over her mouth.* FRANCES *bites his hand.*)
Arrgh! You bit me.

FRANCES: You deserve it.

JACK: You bit my hand. You've drawn blood. Christ! My blood. You. You. Cannibal!
(*A knock. Pause. A knock on the door.*)

FRANCES: Aren't you going to see who's there?

JACK: What?
(*A knock.*)

FRANCES: Dear God! Go and see!
(*After a pause* JACK *goes. Pause. Enter* MILLY.)

JACK: It's Milly.
(*Pause.*)

MILLY: I suppose we should try and deal with this like civilized human beings, but is that possible?
(*Silence.*)

JACK: How did you know we were here?

MILLY: Michael told me.

JACK: Who told Michael?

FRANCES: I did.

JACK: Jesus. What about your cousins?

MILLY: I managed to put them off.

JACK: But where are the kids?

MILLY: They're at Frank and Diana's. They're staying the
night.

JACK: Oh. Lucky Frank and Diana.
(*Pause.*)

MILLY: I felt I had to come. I thought about not coming. I even
thought about pretending I didn't know, but I couldn't see
how that would solve anything. So I decided to come.

JACK: I wish I were dead. I'm so sorry, Milly. I'm so sorry . . .
(*Pause.*)

MILLY: What happened to the beds? Do they always get in such
a state?

JACK: Oh . . . no. We had an accident. No one was hurt.
(*Silence.*)

FRANCES: I think Milly ought to know that it's all over.

MILLY: What's that, Frances?

FRANCES: It's finished.

MILLY: Really?

FRANCES: Yes, it's finished. (*Pause.*) It's just over.

MILLY: How convenient.

FRANCES: He doesn't care about me. He's never cared about
me. He was just after a good time.

JACK: Frances.

FRANCES: It's true, isn't it?

MILLY: (*To* JACK) The point is I trusted you. I actually trusted
you. I thought, he's a good man. He's good to the kids. I
trust him. Then a friend comes to my house and tells me
his wife is having an affair with my husband. (*Brief pause.*)
How long has it been going on, Jack?

JACK: Er . . .

FRANCES: A year.

JACK: Oh.

MILLY: A year? You've been lying to me for a year?

JACK: I haven't been . . .

MILLY: How could you walk into the house and lie? Kiss me on the cheek. Pick up the kids and kiss the kids, and then lie. I can't imagine what it's like in your head. What's going on in there, Jack?

JACK: I don't know.

FRANCES: Of course he knows. He knows I loved him.

MILLY: What?

FRANCES: I've loved him, you know.

MILLY: I don't need to hear anything from you.

FRANCES: Well . . .

MILLY: I don't want to hear! (*Pause.*) You call this love?

FRANCES: Yes, I've loved him a long time. God knows why. But it doesn't matter what I feel. He's managed to put an end to all that. I think he actually cares for you. He probably loves you even though he doesn't know it. He certainly doesn't give a damn about me.

MILLY: He's never loved me.

JACK: Milly . . .

MILLY: You think I don't know that now. We're friends, that's what we are, friends, and it worked. But you don't expect this, do you? Not from your best friend. You don't expect this kind of treament from your best friend. From an enemy? Yes. But your best friend?

JACK: I . . . um . . . nothing.
(*Pause.*)

FRANCES: There's nothing I can say either. Nothing. I'm desperately sorry, Milly. (*Pause.*) What about Michael? How was he? Was he all right? (*Pause.*) Goodbye, Jack.
(FRANCES *exits. Silence.*)

JACK: Milly. I'm shattered. Really. I'm totally shattered. I feel like I'm in little pieces all over the floor.
(*Pause.*)

MILLY: Why?

JACK: What?

MILLY: Why?

JACK: I don't know.

MILLY: You should have talked to me.

JACK: I know.

MILLY: You should have let me help you.

JACK: Well, it is a tricky subject to bring up.

MILLY: You should have trusted me.

JACK: I know I should have.

MILLY: We're supposed to be together. We're supposed to face things together.

JACK: It wasn't anything, Milly. It was just the odd, the occasional afternoon. Milly?

MILLY: Will you help me with this bed.

JACK: Of course I will.

(*They make the beds.*)

MILLY: You think I haven't been tempted?

JACK: You have?

MILLY: Of course I have, Jack.

JACK: Oh.

(*Pause.*)

MILLY: And more than once.

JACK: More than once?

MILLY: Oh, yes. Quite often actually. Straighten that sheet, will you.

JACK: Quite often? (*Laughs.*) Who are these men? Do I know them?

MILLY: Oh, they're just men I've come across and . . .

JACK: What?

MILLY: Well. Sometimes . . .

JACK: Yes?

MILLY: Sometimes I've really fallen for the odd one.

JACK: Fallen?

MILLY: Oh yes, Jack. Sometimes I've really wanted the odd one.

(*Pause.*)

JACK: What are you trying to tell me?

MILLY: Oh, nothing. Except wasn't I the fool. I mean, I should have done it. Don't you think I should have?

JACK: Should have what?

MILLY: You know what I'm talking about!

JACK: Listen, sweetheart, you're my wife!

MILLY: Oh yes! That's why I didn't do it. Because I am your wife. I actually held back for the sake of our marriage. That's a good one, isn't it? You didn't hold back, did you?

JACK: Well, that's not the point.

MILLY: Oh . . . Isn't it?

JACK: Of course it's not the point.

(*Pause*.)

MILLY: Well, I'll tell you something. I'll tell you something for nothing!

JACK: What?

MILLY: If that's not the point I shan't resist any more.

JACK: Shan't resist?

MILLY: To think of the chances I've wasted because of you!

JACK: Who the hell are these men?

MILLY: Oh, they're just men. Men I've talked to. Men I've met and talked to and then they've made a pass.

JACK: A pass!

MILLY: Yes.

JACK: The bastards!

MILLY: I know.

JACK: Who the hell do they think they are, making a pass at my wife!

MILLY: Oh, they're just men, Jack. Men!

JACK: Did they want to go to bed with you?

MILLY: Of course.

JACK: With you?

MILLY: Yes, Jack!

JACK: What about you? Did you want to go to bed with them?

MILLY: Oh, not all of them, Jack.

JACK: Christ! I thought you loved me.

MILLY: Of course I do. That's why I didn't go to bed with anyone.

JACK: But you wanted to?

46

MILLY: Oh, yes.

JACK: Well, that's the same thing!

MILLY: Oh, no, it's not!

JACK: Of course it bloody is, Milly!

MILLY: I found if you leave it alone it eventually goes away. The feeling . . . The desire . . . but I don't think I'll do that the next time. The next time I think I'll treat myself.

JACK: Treat yourself! You've got a bloody nerve telling me all this!

MILLY: But I'm actually grateful for all this. I don't see why you should have all the good times.

JACK: Good times?

MILLY: Why can't we both have good times?

JACK: You call what's happened here this afternoon a good time?

MILLY: Oh. Wasn't it?
(*Pause.*)

JACK: I was just having a little ding dong. A little tumble between the sheets. It's perfectly normal.

MILLY: Normal?

JACK: Well. . . What's normal? Who decides? Eh?

MILLY: I get up each morning and although you see me making breakfast, the truth is I'm really struggling. I'm really struggling to hold it all together. (*Brief pause.*) All for what? So you can have a tumble with Frances?

JACK: Oh, forgive me, Frances.

MILLY: Frances!

JACK: Oh, hell! Milly . . .

MILLY: I was your best friend.

JACK: Milly . . .

MILLY: Take your hands off me!

JACK: I've said I'm sorry. What more do you want?
(MILLY *starts to go.* JACK *blocks her.*)
Where are you going? Are you going home?

MILLY: Home?

JACK: Yes.

MILLY: Home?

47

JACK: Shall we go together?

MILLY: I'm not going home.

JACK: No?

MILLY: No.

JACK: Where are you going? (*Pause.*) Christ! You're not going off with one of those men, are you?

MILLY: Why not?

JACK: Why not? You can't!

MILLY: Oh yes, and what are you going to do about it! (*Pause.*)

JACK: Milly, please come home.

MILLY: We'll have to see, won't we? We'll just have to wait and see.

(MILLY *exits. Pause.* JACK *holds his head.*)

JACK: Oh, hell!

(JACK *stands in anguished silence as the lights fade.*)

THE DAY OF THE DOG

CHARACTERS

ALLEN	forties
CLIFF	forties
MAURICE	early thirties
TERRI	early thirties
VALERIE	early thirties

A pub courtyard by the Thames in South-west London. High summer. Noon.

Blackout. Elvis Presley's 'One Night' plays in the blackout. Lights up. ALLEN *sits at a table. He holds his head. He is hunched over a glass of whisky.* TERRI *and* VALERIE *sit at a distant table.* VALERIE *pulls up her skirt and suns herself.* TERRI *flicks through a glossy magazine. The music swells as* CLIFF *and* MAURICE *enter from the pub. They each have a pint of beer. They listen at the open door until the song ends.* MAURICE *closes the door. Pause.*

CLIFF: Christ, it's hot!

MAURICE: Yeah, it's steamy all right.

CLIFF: Here's to the king. Cheers.

MAURICE: Yeah, the king. There'll never be another.
  (*Sings to himself.*) One night with you . . .

CLIFF: (*Sings.*) Is all I'm praying for . . .
  (*The two women giggle.*)
  Dear God! Look at that.

MAURICE: Oh, yes, please.

CLIFF: What are they up to?

MAURICE: Hi! Hello ladies.
  (*The women ignore* MAURICE.)

CLIFF: My God! They flaunt it everywhere. Everywhere!
  I mean they even flaunt it here.

MAURICE: Well, Why not?
  (MAURICE *approaches the women.*)
  Cheers, ladies. Happy days.
  (*Pause.* MAURICE *moves off. Pause.*)
  I don't believe it.

CLIFF: What?

MAURICE: Well, well, well! Look who's here.

CLIFF: Who?

MAURICE: Allen.

CLIFF: Allen? Where? No! Hey, Allen!

ALLEN: Hello, Cliff.

CLIFF: Dear me, you look appalling. You're not drunk, are
 you?

MAURICE: Allen drunk? Allen's never been drunk in his life.
 Allen's never been drunk, like us ordinary mortals, have
 you, Allen?

ALLEN: Hello, Maurice.

CLIFF: Well, I've never seen Allen in here at this hour and
 that's for sure. My God. How are you? How's tricks?

ALLEN: Oh, I'm all right.

CLIFF: You don't look all right.

ALLEN: Well ... I'm all right, really. I'm all right.

MAURICE: Well, I don't know, Allen. You look pretty ragged
 to me.

ALLEN: Oh, I'm all right you know ... I'm....

CLIFF: Hey, Allen, old son. What is it? What's up?

MAURICE: Hey, Allen? Allen?

CLIFF: Oh, no. Don't tell me, it's the wife.

MAURICE: Cliff!

ALLEN: How did you know?

CLIFF: Well, you know. You've got the haunted look, old son.
 The trapped animal. I smelt it a mile off.

MAURICE: You would.

CLIFF: You see, I know women, Allen. They're vipers.
 (MAURICE *laughs*.)
 I know what I'm talking about, Maurice. I mean, have you
 really clocked those two tarts over there. Look at them,
 Allen.
 (*The three men look at the women.* TERRI *crosses her legs,
 baring a thigh.*)

MAURICE: Oh, come on, Cliff. They're all right.

CLIFF: All right?

MAURICE: Well, I wouldn't say no.

CLIFF: You never say no, do you? That's your trouble. I've never
heard you say no. In fact, no is a word you don't know.

MAURICE: What about you! Hell, the stuff you've been seen
 with. The refugees you've helped across the border!

CLIFF: All right, all right!

MAURICE: Well?

CLIFF: OK! Well ... anyway, cheers, Allen.

MAURICE: Yeah, cheers.

> (MAURICE *and* CLIFF *drink. Pause.*)
> Jesus, it's hot today. Has it ever been this hot? It was hot in
> '75, but it wasn't this hot. I mean, I'm sweating more than
> I drink. Is that possible? (*Sings to himself.*) One night with
> you. Is all I'm praying for ...
> (*Pause.*)

CLIFF: All right, Allen. Let's hear it. What's the woman done?

ALLEN: Oh ... You don't want to know, do you?

CLIFF: Of course I do. It's a hot day. Nothing's happening ...

MAURICE: Nothing ever does.

CLIFF: I'm up for a story. I'm sure Maurice is up for a story.
Aren't you, Maurice?

MAURICE: Oh yeah. I'm always up for a story. (*Under his
breath*) Jesus, Cliff.

ALLEN: (*Agitated*) Well ... You see, as I was making for the
door, as I got to the door, she actually said, you ought to
see a shrink.
(*Pause.*)

CLIFF: Good grief. She said that?

MAURICE: A shrink?

ALLEN: You ought to see a quack.

CLIFF: Christ! She's got a nerve.

ALLEN: I said, you mean a witch doctor? Yes, she said, a witch
doctor. A medicine man.
(*Pause.*)

CLIFF: Women.

MAURICE: They're full of advice.

CLIFF: The air's thick with their advice. I haven't met one who
can't resist having a dig. I mean, who the hell do they think
they are?

ALLEN: I said to her, you can see all the shrinks in the world,
but there is not one who can explain it to you.
(*Pause.*)

CLIFF: You said that?

ALLEN: Yes.

CLIFF: You were trading blows, were you?

ALLEN: Yes, my parting shot, actually it felt like a wild right at the time, well, my parting shot was, there's no use trying to solve riddles that are only riddles for those seeking solutions.
(*Pause.*)

MAURICE: What?

ALLEN: There is no use trying to solve riddles that are only riddles for those seeking solutions.
(*Pause.*)

CLIFF: Well ... I have to say it, Allen ... you were punching the air with that one.

ALLEN: Wasn't I.

MAURICE: All this was at the door, was it?

ALLEN: Yes.

MAURICE: I call that a long exit.

ALLEN: It was, Maurice. It was bad. It was an extreme close-up. Her words following me down the stairs. 'That's what you need. You need a session with the shrink.'
(*Silence.* MAURICE *and* CLIFF *drink.*)

CLIFF: Was it something you'd done? Is that it? I mean, what brought on this outrageous personal attack?

ALLEN: Well ... I ...

MAURICE: You haven't had a dabble, have you?

ALLEN: Well ...

MAURICE: What!

CLIFF: You haven't, have you?

ALLEN: Well, yes ...

MAURICE: I never took you for a dabbler, Allen.

ALLEN: Yes.

CLIFF: Allen's had a dabble! I can't believe it. Who is she?

ALLEN: Well ... I just couldn't help myself.

CLIFF: Couldn't help yourself?

MAURICE: That's a poor excuse.

CLIFF: It's not even an excuse.

ALLEN: I just couldn't resist it.

MAURICE: Who can? I can't.

CLIFF: We all know you can't.

MAURICE: Well, a saint might, but that's why he's a saint. I mean, there's so much of it about.

CLIFF: Are you telling me. What are those two if they're not slags?

MAURICE: Oh, come on, Cliff, they're sunning themselves. They're just picking up a tan.

CLIFF: Picking up a tan! This is a pub for Christ's sake!

MAURICE: All right, all right. We all know what you think. (*Pause.*)

ALLEN: Anyway she was actually over forty.

CLIFF: What?

MAURICE: Past forty?

CLIFF: What are you? A life guard?
(MAURICE *and* CLIFF *laugh. They drink. Pause.*)

CLIFF: So...

MAURICE: Let's have it.

CLIFF: The when.

MAURICE: The how.

CLIFF: The why.

ALLEN: Well... I'd just walked our youngest to the school gates when this woman offered...

MAURICE: One of the mothers?

ALLEN: Yes, I'd actually had a brief chat with her once at a parent–teachers...

MAURICE: Oh...

CLIFF: One of those.

ALLEN: Anyway she offered me a lift.

CLIFF: She has wheels.

MAURICE: I like it.

ALLEN: Yes, she offered me a lift back. It had started to rain. (*Pause.*)

CLIFF: So?

ALLEN: I got into the car...

MAURICE: Shrewd move.

ALLEN: And she puts her hand on my knee.

CLIFF: Oh, no!

MAURICE: Not the knee!

CLIFF: Anything but the knee!

ALLEN: I look at the hand. The knee. Cut to her face. It's smiling.

CLIFF: Well, it would be.

ALLEN: Then it's a close-up on her mouth.

CLIFF: A kiss already?

MAURICE: She's fast.

CLIFF: Fast? No, that's speedy. That's extremely speedy.

ALLEN: No, no. She asks, have you got time for a coffee?

CLIFF: Oh, no! A coffee?

MAURICE: The roasted bean?

CLIFF: Have you got time?

MAURICE: Time is what you've got.

ALLEN: Well, I answer...

    (*Pause.*)

CLIFF: Yes?

ALLEN: Real or instant?

CLIFF: I don't believe it!

MAURICE: Real or instant?

CLIFF: Has this boy got class!

MAURICE: Yeah, you don't catch him throwing it away for a cup of instant.

CLIFF: A real pro, Allen. I like it.

ALLEN: She answers...

CLIFF: I can't bear it!

ALLEN: She answers, will Waitrose Continental Blend do?

MAURICE: Oh, my God.

CLIFF: Continental Blend? Old Allen!

MAURICE: Oh, I don't know, Cliff. It sounds like the real business to me.

    (*Pause.*)

ALLEN: Well ... then there were lots of close-ups in the kitchen. Lots of admiring the knocked-through lounge. The new bay window. Her husband's into DIY.

MAURICE: Always down his shed, is he?

ALLEN: Oh yes, lots of fitted wardrobes and stripped-pine doors.

MAURICE: You got the conducted tour, did you?

ALLEN: Oh yes, I had to work for it.

MAURICE: (*To* CLIFF) It sounds a real sweat to me.
 (*Pause.*)

ALLEN: But then . . .

CLIFF: Ah ha!

MAURICE: The moment itself?

CLIFF: (*To* MAURICE) Extreme close-up in the guest room.

ALLEN: Yes. How did you know?

CLIFF: A wild guess, Allen. A shot in the dark.

ALLEN: Actually . . . it was an extremely extreme close-up indeed.

MAURICE: Oh . . . new frontiers, was it?

ALLEN: Virtually.
 (*Pause.*)

MAURICE: Oh . . .

CLIFF: Good, was it?

ALLEN: Oh, better than good. Oh, way, way beyond good.
 (ALLEN *drinks. Silence.*)

MAURICE: Who is she?

CLIFF: Do we know this woman?

MAURICE: I demand a name.

CLIFF: We both demand a name.

ALLEN: Well . . .
 (*Pause.*)

CLIFF: Aren't you going to share it with your mates?

MAURICE: Mates from way back.

CLIFF: Oh, come on, Allen. We let you play in our team.

MAURICE: Yeah, we let you play in goal.

ALLEN: Oh, all right. Well . . . Jean B . . .

CLIFF: Blair?

ALLEN: Yes.

MAURICE: The solicitor's wife?

ALLEN: Yes.

CLIFF: Oh, no! No! Oh, no!

MAURICE: Not Jean Blair!

ALLEN: Yes.

CLIFF: Oh my God!

(MAURICE *and* CLIFF *laugh.*)

ALLEN: You know her?

CLIFF: I thought I recognized the stripped pine!

ALLEN: You've ... you've been there?

CLIFF: Well ... I can't tell a lie.

ALLEN: Oh...

CLIFF: You've been there too, haven't you, Maurice?

MAURICE: Half of Putney has actually. (*Brief pause.*)
    Sorry.

ALLEN: I didn't know.
    (*Pause.*)

CLIFF: Still...

MAURICE: It passed the morning.

CLIFF: Got you through to lunch.

ALLEN: Oh yes, it did that.

MAURICE: Got you through to your first pint.

CLIFF: Or, in your case, your first scotch.

ALLEN: Oh yes, it certainly did that.
    (*Pause.*)

CLIFF: So. Don't tell me you went and told the wife? Is that it,
    Allen?

MAURICE: Oh yeah, hence the 'witch doctor' line.

ALLEN: Well, actually my wife saw me coming out of the house.
    (*Pause.* MAURICE *and* CLIFF *wince.*)

CLIFF: Oh, no.

MAURICE: That is bad.

CLIFF: That is caught.

MAURICE: I call that caught in the act.

CLIFF: Dear God, that is bad luck.

MAURICE: It's worse than bad luck, it's no luck!
    (MAURICE *and* CLIFF *laugh.*)

CLIFF: (*After a pause.*) Poor old Allen.

MAURICE: You poor sod.

ALLEN: Yes.
 (*Pause.*)
CLIFF: So. What did you say?
MAURICE: How did you cover up?
CLIFF: I hope you didn't try to be funny?
MAURICE: You didn't crack any jokes?
ALLEN: No.
MAURICE: Wise.
CLIFF: Extremely wise.
ALLEN: I thought so at the time.
CLIFF: So?
MAURICE: What did you say?
ALLEN: I told the truth.
 (*Silence.*)
MAURICE: The what?
ALLEN: The truth.
CLIFF: The truth?
ALLEN: Yes.
MAURICE: The actual truth?
ALLEN: Yes, Maurice.
MAURICE: The details?
CLIFF: The actual details of the encounter?
ALLEN: Yes.
CLIFF: My God.
 (MAURICE *and* ALLEN *drink. Pause.*)
MAURICE: The truth?
ALLEN: Yes. It was a mistake.
CLIFF: Mistake!
MAURICE: A serious error!
CLIFF: Oh, Allen!
MAURICE: You idiot!
ALLEN: I knew it the moment I said it. One look into her eyes
 and I knew it.
CLIFF: I mean, Christ! Why didn't you lie, Allen?
ALLEN: I don't know.
CLIFF: Any old lie.
MAURICE: Any old eyewash would have done.

ALLEN: Would it?

CLIFF: Didn't you have your prepared speech?

ALLEN: My what?

MAURICE: Your emergency speech for such an encounter.

ALLEN: What speech?

MAURICE: You dummy.

CLIFF: Oh, Allen, never be without your speech.

MAURICE: Anything to buy time.

CLIFF: Like, oh hello, darling, what are you doing in this neck of the woods? I didn't know you knew anyone round here. You should have told me you were coming this way. We could have come together . . .

MAURICE: Never let her interrupt. Never let her stop your flow.

CLIFF: By the way, who is it you're seeing? Do I know them? Actually I'm only here by chance. I had to help this old lady into her house. Poor old dear. She fell over at the crossing. I helped her home. She was really shaken. How does that sound?

MAURICE: Not bad for you.

ALLEN: Not bad? It was awful.

CLIFF: Well, it usually works.

MAURICE: Then of course it's offensive time. Like, why don't I come with you, darling, now that I'm here, and by the way, who are you seeing?

CLIFF: Because you never know.

ALLEN: You mean . . .

CLIFF: Precisely.

MAURICE: Well, you were in with someone's wife.

CLIFF: Who's in with yours?

(*Pause.*)

ALLEN: Well, not me. Not any more.

CLIFF: Oh, no!

MAURICE: She hasn't, has she?

CLIFF: Oh, she hasn't gone and given you the old elbow, has she?

ALLEN: I thought she'd respect me if I told the truth.

(MAURICE *and* CLIFF *laugh.*)

MAURICE: I cannot believe my ears.

CLIFF: It's beyond belief!

MAURICE: The truth is the last thing she wants to hear. She doesn't want to know. She might think you are, you know, having a dabble, but she doesn't want to know you're having a dabble.

CLIFF: Oh, good Lord, no. If she knows you're having a dabble, well, she has to face it. If she knows you're dabbling the poor woman is presented with a series of appalling insights.

MAURICE: Like, why's he having a dabble with someone else?

CLIFF: Aren't I enough?

MAURICE: Aren't I good enough?

CLIFF: What does she have that I haven't got?

MAURICE: Every time he goes out . . . is he having a dabble?

CLIFF: Am I the kind of wife who doesn't mind having a dabbler for a husband?

MAURICE: Exactly. Am I a sucker?

CLIFF: But if she doesn't know you like a dabble . . . well . . . it's business as usual.

MAURICE: It's, hello darling, had a nice day? Close-up. Peck on cheek. We've got stuffed aubergines for supper.

CLIFF: Instead of no supper.

MAURICE: Or supper on the wall.

CLIFF: Or aubergine over the face.

(MAURICE *and* CLIFF *laugh. They drink. Pause.*)

ALLEN: (*Anguished*) What have I done? What have I done? (*Pause.*)

MAURICE: Well . . .

CLIFF: You've done what we all do.

MAURICE: That's what we do.

CLIFF: Except . . .

MAURICE: You blew it.

CLIFF: I mean, rule number one.

MAURICE: If you're going to do it.

CLIFF: Do it far from home.

MAURICE: In another town.

CLIFF: Another country.

MAURICE: Another language.

CLIFF: That you can't speak.

MAURICE: Give a false name.

CLIFF: That can't be traced.

MAURICE: A false personal history.

CLIFF: A totally false person actually.

MAURICE: Instead of which . . .

CLIFF: You do it . . .

MAURICE: With the mother of a child at your kid's school.

CLIFF: In her house.

MAURICE: In broad daylight.

CLIFF: In a street.

MAURICE: In which your wife is loitering.

(MAURICE *and* CLIFF *laugh*.)

ALLEN: I got carried away.

(MAURICE *and* CLIFF *howl with laughter*.)

CLIFF: Never get carried away!

ALLEN: I wanted her.

MAURICE: Oh, no! No.

CLIFF: Mistake. Mistake.

MAURICE: *Never* get carried away. *Never* want her.

CLIFF: That's the quickest route to the funny farm.

MAURICE: Because you'll want her again.

CLIFF: And then, speaking from experience, it really begins.

MAURICE: Oh right, it's all phone calls.

CLIFF: Late back from work.

MAURICE: Damp hotel rooms.

CLIFF: Constant lies.

MAURICE: A bloody web of lies.

CLIFF: And of course she'll want more.

MAURICE: She'll want to be seen out with you.

CLIFF: She'll moan she's not getting enough of you.

MAURICE: Then she'll want you to divorce your wife.

CLIFF: And marry her.

MAURICE: And of course if you do marry her . . . you'll be back to square one.

CLIFF: And all the lies start again. (*Brief pause.*)
Bloody hell! All for what?
(*Pause.*)

MAURICE: A minute.

CLIFF: Oh, come on, two minutes.

MAURICE: Oh, all right, two minutes. If you're lucky.
(*Pause.*)

CLIFF: Two lousy minutes! It makes me sick. All that energy
for two stinking minutes. We must be mad.
(*Pause.*)

ALLEN: I couldn't help it. I don't know why. She was . . .

MAURICE: Oh, we know. We know Jean.

ALLEN: But you broke the rules.

MAURICE: What's the point of rules if you can't break them?

CLIFF: The point is, Allen, we didn't get caught.

ALLEN: I just had no control. I couldn't resist her.

CLIFF: Neither could I.

MAURICE: Me neither.

CLIFF: There's something about a forty-year-old woman. They
appreciate it. They know they haven't got much time left so
they grab it while they can.

MAURICE: Oh yeah, there's a certain urgency, a certain relish, a
certain devil-may-care attitude.
(*Pause.*)

CLIFF: It's quite appealing actually.

MAURICE: We do sympathize.

CLIFF: It's just bad luck.

MAURICE: Awfully bad luck. Got a cigarette?
(*Pause.*)

ALLEN: What am I going to do?

CLIFF: Do?

ALLEN: Yes, what am I going to do?

MAURICE: Well . . . the world is your oyster! You have the
field before you.

CLIFF: You can play it without guilt.

MAURICE: Without hindrance.

ALLEN: That's not what I want.

MAURICE: No?

ALLEN: I don't want that.

MAURICE: You're joking, of course.

ALLEN: I want my wife.

MAURICE: Oh Christ, I can't cope with this, Allen.

ALLEN: I want to be with my wife.

MAURICE: This is definitely not on, old son.

ALLEN: I love her.

CLIFF: Love? Love?

ALLEN: I love her.

MAURICE: But, Allen, you've got it made.

ALLEN: I enjoy my marriage!

CLIFF: I don't believe it.

ALLEN: Well, I did.

MAURICE: Who enjoys marriage for Christ's sake?

ALLEN: I love my kids. What's going to happen to my kids?

MAURICE: Oh, well, she'll get them, of course.

CLIFF: They always do.

MAURICE: You'll get no sympathy.

CLIFF: She'll get the house too.

MAURICE: You'll be out of pocket there you know.

CLIFF: He hasn't got a chance. I lost mine, didn't I? I got took to the cleaners. I'll tell you what I'd do. I'd give her the lot and be done with it before the blood starts to flow.

MAURICE: It'll be his blood, too. You know women. He hasn't got a hope in hell. (*To* ALLEN) I wouldn't like to be in your shoes, Allen, when the blood starts to flow.
(*Pause.*)

ALLEN: I was walking with my little girl. We were walking along a road. She was holding my hand, and I thought, you're walking along with your little girl. Remember it. Her little hand. This little person beside me. She was singing a nursery rhyme . . . I feel as if I'm about to topple.

CLIFF: I think you'd better get the drinks in, Maurice.

MAURICE: Yeah.

ALLEN: I can't even remember where Oxford Street is any more.

(*Pause.*)

MAURICE: (*To* CLIFF) What's he going on about?

CLIFF: Just get the drinks, Mo.

ALLEN: What have I done, Cliff?

CLIFF: Maurice is just getting the drinks in, Allen. OK?

MAURICE: Hell, it's hot today.

(MAURICE *takes off his shirt.*)

CLIFF: Oh no, you're not taking off your shirt. Oh look at this, Allen. What is it all coming to, that's what I want to know? This is a bloody pub, Maurice, not a topless beach!

MAURICE: Clock this and learn.

(MAURICE *swaggers over to* TERRI *and* VALERIE.)
Hello, ladies. I thought I'd join you. You know, catch the old tan. (*Sings.*) One night with you. Is all I'm asking for ... (*Pause.*) Oh, please yourselves.

(MAURICE *exits into the pub.* TERRI *and* VALERIE *smile at each other.*)

CLIFF: Did you see that? Who do those bitches think they are?

ALLEN: I've always been good on directions. I was a good map reader. I don't even know where north is now.

CLIFF: It's OK, Allen. Calm down. It's OK.

ALLEN: Don't tell me it's OK when it's not OK. It's not OK! (*Pause. The faint sound of music from the pub. Bruce Springsteen's 'Dancing in the Dark'.*)

CLIFF: It takes time, Allen. Well ... in my case, after the bitch left me, I should say, well ... a couple of years.

ALLEN: (*Shocked*) A couple of years?

CLIFF: Yes. (*Pause.*) Still, it soon passes, and in a year or so you'll wonder what the fuss was all about. You'll be laughing at something, having a good howl in a pub or somewhere, when suddenly you'll find it impossible to remember her face.

ALLEN: What?

CLIFF: Oh yes, it soon passes. (*Pause.*) Anyway what woman is worth it? Christ! They think they've got it all sewn up. They have their babies and they've got it all sewn up. Not only that, they don't really need us afterwards. We're just an inconvenience. We're just a lump hanging round the house. A thing in the corner. That's what we are. Something to humour, in case one day, one distant day, one far-off day, they just might get bored with their kids and come looking for us to pass the time of day.

ALLEN: Is that what you think?

CLIFF: Killing a man is killing a man. Some prefer to call it marriage. You're well out of it.

ALLEN: I liked my marriage.

CLIFF: Then you shouldn't have dabbled.

(*The music swells up as* MAURICE *enters through the door. He carries the drinks.*)

Oh no, here he comes!

(MAURICE *bops along to the song.*)

MAURICE: Listen to this, ladies. That's old Bruce blasting out. (*Pause.*)

VALERIE: (*Taking off her sunglasses*) Who?

MAURICE: Ah ha. Bruce. The boss. Bruce Springsteen.

TERRI: Who's he?

MAURICE: What? You've never heard of him?

VALERIE: No.

MAURICE: You really haven't heard of old Bruce?

TERRI: No.

MAURICE: Are you taking the piss?

(TERRI *and* VALERIE *laugh.*)

You are taking the piss. Listen ladies, I like it.

(MAURICE *sits at their table.*)

CLIFF: Look at that, Allen. He just can't leave it alone. What the hell is he up to? Is he trying to pull those tarts or what? Allen?

ALLEN: What?

CLIFF: Look at him. What's he up to?

ALLEN: Why don't you go over and join him, Cliff?

CLIFF: What?

ALLEN: Go over.

CLIFF: Me? Go over?

ALLEN: Yes, you're dying to go over.

CLIFF: Oh, that's a good one, isn't it? That's a good one.

ALLEN: Oh, for Christ's sake go over, will you!

CLIFF: Well . . . OK. All right. If that's how you feel. (*Pause. Calls.*) Hey! You!

MAURICE: Who? Me?

CLIFF: Yes. You.

MAURICE: Are you talking to me?

CLIFF: Where's my pint?

MAURICE: Here.

> (*The two women laugh.*)
> (*To* VALERIE) You'll just love Cliff.

CLIFF: This shouldn't take long, Allen. I won't be a minute. (CLIFF *saunters over*.) So? What's going on here? (MAURICE *sits next to* TERRI.)

MAURICE: This is Terri, Cliff.

CLIFF: Terry?

TERRI: Teresa.

CLIFF: Oh, right. Whatever suits you.

TERRI: Yes.

MAURICE: And this is . . .

VALERIE: Valerie. (*She holds out her hand.*) Hello, Cliff.

CLIFF: Oh. Hello. Valerie.

VALERIE: Why don't you sit down? Here.

CLIFF: Sit down?

VALERIE: You don't have to.

MAURICE: (*Abruptly*) Sit down, Cliff.

CLIFF: (*Looking back at* ALLEN) Right. (CLIFF *sits*.)

MAURICE: The ladies were just saying . . .

VALERIE: We were just saying, that it's about time we had something to eat.

CLIFF: What?

MAURICE: It's lunchtime, Cliff. You remember lunchtime.

VALERIE: We thought, for a change, we'd try a kebab.

CLIFF: A kebab?

MAURICE: Yes, Cliff, you know, a doner.

CLIFF: Oh.

VALERIE: There's a new place just opened up by the lights on the Upper Richmond Road. We thought we'd give it a whirl.

CLIFF: Oh, right. A whirl.

(*Pause.*)

MAURICE: (*To* CLIFF) Are you with us?

VALERIE: Would you like to take us?

CLIFF: Take you?

MAURICE: Yes, Cliff. The ladies are hungry!

CLIFF: All right. It sounds OK to me.

VALERIE: Good. Let's go.

(*The women prepare to leave.*)

CLIFF: What?

VALERIE: Let's go.

CLIFF: Wait. Listen. I'll have to get Allen.

MAURICE: Oh, no!

CLIFF: No?

MAURICE: You can't bring him along. I can't be doing with all that.

CLIFF: Look, Maurice, we just can't leave him.

MAURICE: Why not? You know how it is, ladies. Old Allen over there got caught by the wife, and now he's in a right old state about it. What can we do?

(*Pause. They look at* ALLEN.)

VALERIE: He looks the type.

TERRI: He's not our type.

MAURICE: Oh, no! He's certainly not your type.

TERRI: Why get in such a state? Over what?

MAURICE: I couldn't agree more, darlin'.

CLIFF: Well. Maybe she's right.

MAURICE: Of course she's right, Cliff! Christ!

CLIFF: All right, all right, but what do I say to him?

MAURICE: You don't have to say anything. He doesn't even know we're here.

VALERIE: What's the problem, Cliff?

CLIFF: Well . . .

VALERIE: All we have to do is walk out. It's not our problem.

TERRI: Are you sure you two are up for it?

MAURICE: What! Are we up for it!

VALERIE: Well, then. Let's shift it.

(TERRI *and* VALERIE *exit.* MAURICE *drains his pint. He checks his money. He exits running. Pause.* CLIFF *puts his pint down. He places* ALLEN'*s scotch on the floor quite close to* ALLEN. CLIFF *exits. The lights fade.* ALLEN *is caught in a single spot. He is in despair.*)

BLACKOUT

COMMITMENT

CHARACTERS

ELLIS   middle thirties
JOANNA   early thirties
JULIA   early thirties

The half-decorated kitchen of a terraced house in West London. Early evening.

*John Lennon's song, 'Nobody Told Me' from the 'Milk and Honey'
album is heard over the auditorium speakers.*
ELLIS *enters at the beginnng of the first chorus. He is listening to the
same song on his Walkman. He carries a disposable nappy. He
drops the nappy in the bin as he sings the last line of the chorus,
'Strange days indeed'. He gets a bottle of wine and glass and sits at
the table and pours himself a drink.*
JOANNA *enters during the second verse. She is daunted by the untidy
kitchen.* ELLIS *sings the last line of the second chorus, 'Most
peculiar Mama'. He blows* JOANNA *a kiss.*
JOANNA *starts to clean up.*
ELLIS *switches off his Walkman at the end of the song.*
Silence.
ELLIS: Is he asleep?
JOANNA: (*Mocks.*) Is he asleep? Of course he's asleep. Would I
    be here if he wasn't asleep? (*Pause.*) Oh, I'm so tired
    tonight. How can a two-year-old child do this to me?
ELLIS: He won't be two for ever, Jo.
JOANNA: Look at me, Ellis.
ELLIS: Oh don't start up tonight.
JOANNA: I used to be young once.
ELLIS: So did I.
JOANNA: I used to stay up all night and think nothing of it.
    What's happened to me?
ELLIS: You're just tired.
JOANNA: Tired? I'm whacked. I'm virtually out on my feet.
ELLIS: You think I can't see that? I can see you look . . .
JOANNA: Awful?
ELLIS: No.
JOANNA: I know I look awful.
ELLIS: I never said you looked awful.
JOANNA: If you think this is awful, you should see some of the
    mothers at the play group. The ones with two or three kids.

73

You should see their faces. Their eyes. They haven't slept
for years. Years!
(*Pause.*)

ELLIS: What a life. (*He pours another drink.*) Cheers, Jo.

JOANNA: I don't know how they do it, and some of them
actually do it on their own. When they've finally got their
kids to bed they've still got a house to clear up. At least I've
got you. At least you do the washing up.

ELLIS: Ah, well . . .

JOANNA: Oh no, don't tell me you haven't done the washing up.

ELLIS: I was going to.

JOANNA: You said you'd do the washing up.

ELLIS: I fancied a drink first.

JOANNA: You mean to say, you sat here drinking with all that
stuff still in the sink?

ELLIS: I know it looks like that, but I was going to do it.

JOANNA: Oh, Ellis.

ELLIS: I'll do it if you want me to.
    (JOANNA *rises.*)
    Sit down, Jo.

JOANNA: Someone's got to do it.

ELLIS: Why?

JOANNA: I've been at it all day. All day!

ELLIS: All right, all right.

JOANNA: When I've put Sam to bed I don't want to come down
here and find there's still more work. How do you think I
can relax with all that stuff sitting there in the sink?

ELLIS: I can manage it.

JOANNA: Oh, you're a past master at it.

ELLIS: I wanted a drink. What's wrong with a quiet drink? I've
been working too, you know. Where are you going, Jo?

JOANNA: Oh, don't bother yourself. I'm only going to do a spot
of light washing up.

ELLIS: No you're not! You sit still. I'll do it.

JOANNA: You won't.

ELLIS: I'll do it! All right? I'll do the washing up. That is final!
    (*Silence.*)

JOANNA: When?

ELLIS: What?

JOANNA: When?

ELLIS: When what?

JOANNA: When are you going to do it?

ELLIS: When I've had a drink.

JOANNA: You had a drink while I was putting Sam to bed.

ELLIS: Oh, Christ Almighty! (*He leaps up.*) All right. I'll do it now. (*He starts to wash up. Pause.*)

JOANNA: Why is it whenever you do something for me, you make it look like a huge favour?

ELLIS: I queue in Safeways! Every Saturday I queue at that bloody delicatessen counter!

JOANNA: It's still a huge favour. You knew I was upstairs putting Sam to bed. The last lap. Why couldn't you pull your weight and do the stinking washing up! It's only fair.

ELLIS: All right! All right! It's all my fault! I should have done the washing up, but I didn't! I sat down and had a drink. OK? I'm at fault. I'm a pig! I know. Blah, blah, blah! (*Silence.*) Oh, hell.

JOANNA: This is happening too often. (*Pause.*) What's wrong, Ellis?

ELLIS: We take it too seriously, Looking after Sam. We're too serious about it.

JOANNA: But if we don't take it seriously, who will? We agreed to do it properly. What's the point of having a child if you don't give it all you've got? (*Brief pause.*) Well?

ELLIS: I know we agreed, but it's not much fun, is it?

JOANNA: Fun?

ELLIS: Yes, fun. Where's the fun?

JOANNA: It's there if you care to look.

ELLIS: I can't remember the last time we had fun. I didn't bargain for this, you know.

JOANNA: No?

ELLIS: Well, we used to have fun before. We used to go out with friends. Have a chat. Have a laugh. A few drinks . . . and before that . . .

75

JOANNA: There was a time before that?

ELLIS: Well, you forget what you were like.

JOANNA: What do you mean?

ELLIS: Well, you know. You were, well ... you wouldn't hesitate ...

JOANNA: Ah, we're talking about sex, are we?

ELLIS: You couldn't keep your hands off me before.

JOANNA: You're talking about the time before Sam?

ELLIS: Yes.

JOANNA: Before the birth?

ELLIS: Yes.

JOANNA: All right, what are you trying to tell me?

ELLIS: Nothing.

JOANNA: Oh yes, you are.

ELLIS: We had fun. That's all.

JOANNA: And it's not fun now?

ELLIS: I didn't mean that. It's different now. Better.

JOANNA: (*After a pause.*) I don't have any time. I'm up to my neck in nappies and food and dirty clothes. That kind of thing doesn't make you feel very sexy.

ELLIS: Well, it was just fun before. It was fun. Starting out was fun, wasn't it? Well, you were pretty free with it. I remember you behind that garage.

JOANNA: Garage? What garage? I never went behind a garage with you.

ELLIS: You did. You lay down on my mac and I lay down and ...

JOANNA: I never went behind a garage with you. It must have been some other woman. I never lay down on a mac with you and got laid.

ELLIS: (*After a brief pause.*) Are you sure?

JOANNA: She must have been good for you to remember.

ELLIS: Well, it was good, but it wasn't on a mac. No, it was on a coat. My overcoat. That one I bought in Brighton. That second-hand coat I got in the Lanes.

JOANNA: What? That old blue thing?

ELLIS: Yes.

76

JOANNA: The one two sizes too big?

ELLIS: Yes.

JOANNA: The one you had to roll up the sleeves to see your hands?

ELLIS: Yes!

JOANNA: We did it on that?

ELLIS: Yes! No! We weren't on it. We were under it.

JOANNA: Oh, yes. I remember.

ELLIS: What did we look like? What did we think we were up to?

JOANNA: Oh we knew.

ELLIS: Oh yes, we knew all right. We were in a park, not behind a garage. St James's Park, and under two coats.

JOANNA: My mac!

ELLIS: I knew there was a mac somewhere.

JOANNA: Mmmnn. You were right. I couldn't keep my hands off you.

ELLIS: This is more like it.
    (*They cuddle.*)

JOANNA: Oh, those were the days. We had so much time. What did we do with all that time?

ELLIS: Well, we used to lie in every weekend.

JOANNA: Oh don't. A lie in. What I wouldn't give for a lie in, and to read the Sunday papers in bed.

ELLIS: And afterwards?

JOANNA: Oh yes, afterwards.

ELLIS: It's gone too fast. It seems like yesterday.

JOANNA: You must be joking. Yesterday Sam was sick.

ELLIS: Ah, yes.

JOANNA: I had to deal with it and you know how I can't stand sick. He was sick over the sheets. I had to change the sheets twice. He was terrified of the doctor. The doctor kept pulling faces to make Sam laugh except the doctor's face was ugly, and it was even uglier when he pulled a stupid face. In the end we had to hold Sam down while he looked in his mouth. That's what happened yesterday.
    (*Pause.*)

ELLIS: Oh, have a drink, Jo. Forget it.

JOANNA: It's too early to drink.

ELLIS: What?

JOANNA: It's not even seven.

ELLIS: So what?

JOANNA: I'm not going to start drinking this early.

ELLIS: Listen, we used to drink before seven before. We used to drink lots of drinks before seven, and talk with friends. They'd all be round here talking and drinking my drink.

JOANNA: (*Mocks*) And laughing.

ELLIS: Yes, and laughing. They were the days.
(*He drinks. Pause.*)

JOANNA: I wonder what they're all up to tonight?

ELLIS: Oh, that's easy. They're all out having fun.

JOANNA: You think so?

ELLIS: Oh yes. I expect they're out having a bloody good time. You know, on the razzle. (*He drinks.*) Why don't we ask them round here? They could be round here having their fun. They could drink their drinks round here.

JOANNA: Well, we'd have to buy some glasses.

ELLIS: What?

JOANNA: We haven't got enough glasses.

ELLIS: Oh well, that puts an end to it, doesn't it? If we haven't got any glasses, that puts an end to it!

JOANNA: I didn't mean it like that.

ELLIS: Haven't got any glasses! What's the matter with us? We've had it! Do you realize it's like this all the way to the end? I've got to the point. I've got to the point where I actually think, I actually think, thank God that's another day gone. I find that bloody alarming.

JOANNA: The truth is, you don't enjoy domestic life.

ELLIS: Domestic life? Is that what it's called?

JOANNA: You just wish you were somewhere else.

ELLIS: No. The truth is, we've forgotten how to have fun. It's all his fault.

JOANNA: You can't blame Sam. We made Sam. You can't blame him.

78

ELLIS: They're not idiots. They don't have kids hanging round their necks. They're out having a good time. That's where we should be. We should get out and have fun before it's too late. We should get out.

JOANNA: What about Sam? What if he wakes up when we're out? What if he really needs me? What will he feel when he finds some strange person leaning over his bed? What will he feel, Ellis?

ELLIS: We should go out for a meal. We should see a film. Go into town, see a film, have a meal.

JOANNA: Well, if that's what you want, I'd be just as happy if we had people here. That way if Sam needed me I'd be here.

ELLIS: Is that what you want?

JOANNA: Yes, I'd be just as happy to talk to friends here.
(*Pause.*)

ELLIS: We haven't got any friends.

JOANNA: Oh, come off it, Ellis. We've got friends.

ELLIS: We've hardly seen a soul since we had Sam.

JOANNA: That's not true. We know people. We have got a phonebook.
(ELLIS *drinks. Pause.*)

ELLIS: Anyway, talk about what?

JOANNA: Well, just talk. Entertain each other. Discuss events. Listen to what people have to say. Feel alive. I don't know.

ELLIS: You know what they have to say, don't you? You've heard it before. We've all heard it all before.

JOANNA: Well, I would like to hear it all again. I want to talk to people.

ELLIS: OK. Get on the phone. Ask someone round.

JOANNA: (*After a brief pause.*) Now?

ELLIS: Yes, now.

JOANNA: Well ... who shall I call?

ELLIS: Who do we like?

JOANNA: Well ... Dave and Julia, they're the only ones we know with kids.

ELLIS: Why does it have to be couples with kids? Can't we invite single people?

JOANNA: I like Dave and Julia.

ELLIS: All right, phone them up.

JOANNA: This minute?

ELLIS: It's only a phone call, Joanna. We're not actually going out there. It's just a phone call. We must get used to making phone calls.

JOANNA: All right, all right, but we'll have to get some glasses. (*She dials.*)

ELLIS: We'll get glasses. We'll go out tomorrow and buy some glasses.

JOANNA: And forks.

ELLIS: What?

JOANNA: I'd like some new forks. We haven't got enough side plates either.

ELLIS: How much is this going to cost?

JOANNA: It's ringing. (*Pause.*) It's still ringing.

ELLIS: They're probably in the bath.

JOANNA: At this hour?

ELLIS: They're probably soaking in a tub of goat's milk. (*Pause.*)

JOANNA: There's no answer.

ELLIS: Give it another second.

JOANNA: No. There's no one there. No. (*Pause.*)

ELLIS: Well . . . That's a blow!

JOANNA: I expect they're out.

ELLIS: Well, that's that.

JOANNA: At least we tried. (*Silence.*)

ELLIS: Out? What are they doing out at this hour? They've got kids. I mean, they've got two kids.

JOANNA: They've also got help.

ELLIS: Help? I didn't know they had help.

JOANNA: Oh yes, they've had help for ages.

ELLIS: What about the kids?

JOANNA: Oh, I often meet the kids with the help at the play group. She lives in the house. Actually she's quite a big girl, you know. Very good-looking. Doesn't know a thing about kids though.

(*Pause.*)

ELLIS: You know what they're doing, don't you?

JOANNA: What?

ELLIS: They're out having fun.

JOANNA: No.

ELLIS: Oh yes, they're probably out there having affairs.

JOANNA: Affairs? No.

ELLIS: Why not? Everyone else is.

JOANNA: Are they?

ELLIS: Of course they are.

JOANNA: (*After a brief pause.*) We're not.

ELLIS: No.

JOANNA: We're not having affairs.

ELLIS: Christ!

JOANNA: What?

ELLIS: Why aren't we having affairs?

JOANNA: (*Laughing*) Oh, Ellis!

ELLIS: What's wrong with us? What are we doing sitting in this kitchen . . .

JOANNA: In this half-finished kitchen . . .

ELLIS: I'll get round to it. I'll get round to it.

JOANNA: Of course you will.

ELLIS: We're actually sitting here waiting for Sam to wake when we could be out there having a bloody fine affair.

JOANNA: (*Abruptly*) Ellis!

ELLIS: Well . . .

JOANNA: Well what?

ELLIS: Oh, I don't know . . . I don't know what makes us think we should be any different.

(*Pause.*)

JOANNA: (*Laughs.*) We must have read the wrong books.

ELLIS: If I hadn't have read that *Primal Scream*. That was a big mistake that book. It's made me think every time he cries he's having a trauma.

JOANNA: Yes, except it's not Sam who's having the trauma.

ELLIS: It's made us take it far too seriously. There's no guarantee he'll be any better for it. We never got all this attention. We just got dumped on and look at us.

JOANNA: Precisely.

ELLIS: Oh, we're all right. Anyway, that's what they all tell us. 'You turned out all right, didn't you? What are you going on about?'

JOANNA: No. I can't forget so easily. My memories are of partings. Of schools and strange faces. Of girls coughing in the dark, and distant relatives at odd weekends. When I wanted them they were never there. They were away. Doing something important, like taking a holiday. I vowed I'd never do that to my child.

ELLIS: But it's boring me to death!

JOANNA: We have so much.

ELLIS: This business, you know, this kids business, it's overrated!
(*Pause.*)

JOANNA: I never expected to hear you say that.

ELLIS: Well, I've said it, and I've been thinking it for a long time.

JOANNA: What else is there apart from what we have? We have love. We have a child. We have our health. There isn't anything else.

ELLIS: But nothing ever happens, does it! Sam throws up occasionally. I throw up occasionally. But nothing ever happens.

JOANNA: Like what?

ELLIS: Like something unexpected. There's no fun any more. Something is missing, Jo. This can't be it.

JOANNA: Oh yes, it is, Ellis. This is it, and we are living it.
(*Silence.* ELLIS *drinks.*)
I'll never forget that moment after the birth when he snuggled up on to my breast.

ELLIS: Oh, my God.

JOANNA: It was the most complete moment of my life.
(*Pause.*)

ELLIS: No one ever tells you.

JOANNA: What?

ELLIS: What it's like, you know, with a child.

JOANNA: Oh, come on, you can't blame the kids. It's not their fault. Well, not all the time.

ELLIS: It's not having time, that's what it is.

JOANNA: We have time now.

ELLIS: That's true.

JOANNA: I'm too tired to have time now. I want time when I'm up for it. I don't want time when I'm whacked.

ELLIS: Oh, I don't know.

JOANNA: Of course you don't know. Who knows why they have children. It's just something you do. I mean, if you did know beforehand, you know, how they wreck everything, like being together, having a chat, making love when we feel like it, well. Oh no, there they are, butting in, making mad dashes for your legs, scratching your eyes out if you don't give them every second of your time. Well, if we knew...

ELLIS: I'm just not taken with children. I can't get into their world. I find it all one big bloody effort.

JOANNA: Well, I'm not that taken either.

ELLIS: You're not?

JOANNA: No. Other people's children bore me. But Sam, well...

ELLIS: Yes, Sam's different.

JOANNA: Of course he is and he is ours. That is something, Ellis. We are doing it. No one else is doing it for us. It can never be taken away from us that we did it. Oh, I know we could be out. We could be out having fun. We could dump him on someone. Because when you're out you don't hear the crying. You don't see the tears.

ELLIS: In fact when you're out you even forget you've got a child. I know I do.

JOANNA: We made this decision, Ellis. We made it. We're here. Now we've jolly well got to live with it.

(*Pause.*)

ELLIS: And then what?

JOANNA: What do you mean?

ELLIS: The years after Sam. After he's taken one look at us and decided we're middle-aged and boring?

JOANNA: Well, we just grow old together and one of us dies, and the other will be left with good memories.

ELLIS: I can't cope with this, Jo. Pensioners queuing in the supermarket? Is that it? Through thick and thin?

JOANNA: It looks like it.

ELLIS: There must be more.

JOANNA: Yes, to grow into each other.

ELLIS: What about fun? Year after year in the same bed? Between the same sheets?

JOANNA: I'm afraid so.

ELLIS: (*After a brief pause.*) What makes you so sure?

JOANNA: I believe. I have faith.
  (*The doorbell rings.*)

ELLIS: My God, what's that?

JOANNA: It's the doorbell.

ELLIS: Oh no, not the doorbell.

JOANNA: Yes, someone must be at the front door.

ELLIS: Who?

JOANNA: Go and find out.

ELLIS: Someone is actually at our front door! Someone has come to see us!

JOANNA: Oh, go and open the door, will you!
  (ELLIS *exits.* JOANNA *cleans up.*)

ELLIS: (*Off*) No!

JOANNA: Who is it?

ELLIS: (*Off*) Julia. It's Julia!
  (ELLIS *and* JULIA *enter.*)

JOANNA: Julia! Goodness. We just this minute tried to phone you. How strange. We thought it was about time we saw a few friends. So we phoned you, but you were out. So we gave up. It is nice to see you.

ELLIS: How are you, Julia? I must say, you look ravishing.

JOANNA: You do, you know. How much did that dress cost?

84

JULIA: Yes, we were going out tonight.

JOANNA: We thought as much when you didn't answer the phone.

ELLIS: Yes, we thought you were out having fun. You know, fun.

JOANNA: (*Under her breath*) Ellis.

JULIA: But instead of going out Dave decided to tell me he was having an affair.
(*Pause.*)

ELLIS: Oh, Christ.

JULIA: He's gone, Joanna. He's left the boys. He's left me. He's gone off with Bernice.

JOANNA: Your help?

JULIA: Yes, Bernice the help. They've gone off somewhere. No explanation. Nothing. They've just gone.
(*Pause.*)

JOANNA: Come on, Julia. Sit down. Get another glass, Ellis.

ELLIS: Yes, right.
(*He pours a drink.* JULIA *drinks.*)

JULIA: Peter, my youngest, has chicken-pox. He was sick in the hall. It stinks. I've been down on my hands and knees, but I can't seem to get rid of the smell. I can smell it all over the house. (*Brief pause.*) I don't think it's fair, do you? The boys are asking for their father. They want him, but he's not there. He's off with that bitch. Bernice. (*Brief pause.*) What am I supposed to say to them? That their father would rather be with Bernice than his own boys? (*Pause.*) I don't think I'm going to be able to cope. My mother's come too. God help me. She couldn't wait to get over. She brought a case. And if you two don't stop holding hands I think I'll scream!
(SAM *calls 'Mummy' on the child intercom.*) Oh hell, I've gone and woken your Sam.

JOANNA: Oh, that's OK Julia. He probably wants a drink. I'll go.

ELLIS: No, darling, I'll go. You stay with Julia.

JOANNA: No, I'll go.

85

ELLIS: Well, let's both go. We might have to change the sheets.
    You never know.

JOANNA: (*Decisively*) I think you should stay, Ellis.

ELLIS: Ah. OK. I'll stay with Julia. Right.

JOANNA: I won't be a minute, Julia. Have another drink. Why
    don't you pour Julia another drink, Ellis?
    (JOANNA *exits*. ELLIS *pours another drink. Silence.*)

ELLIS: Well . . . old Dave's done a runner, has he?
    (JULIA *stares at* ELLIS.)
    Oh . . . you never know, Julia, he might come back.
    (*Pause.*)

JULIA: Do you find me attractive?

ELLIS: What?

JULIA: I know men like to fool around, but not Dave. I thought
    Dave was different. You're not like that, are you?

ELLIS: Who? Me? Oh, no!

JULIA: Is it just sex? Is that it? Is it just because she's got big
    tits?

ELLIS: (*After a brief pause.*) Oh, that's an awesome question,
    Julia.

JOANNA: (*Calls over the intercom.*) Sam needs a drink, Ellis.
    Bring his feeder up, will you?

ELLIS: Um . . . Sam needs his feeder . . . I have to take it.
    (JULIA *drinks.*)
    There's another bottle in the cupboard if you want it. OK?
    Won't be a tick.
    (ELLIS *exits. Pause.* JULIA *listens to them soothing* SAM *on the*
    intercom. Pause. JULIA *exits. The soothing sounds stop. Pause.*
    JOANNA *enters.*)

JOANNA: Julia? Where are you? Julia? Ellis!

ELLIS: (*Off*) What is it?

JOANNA: Julia's gone. She's gone.
    (*Pause.* ELLIS *enters.*)

ELLIS: She's gone?

JOANNA: We shouldn't have left her.
    (ELLIS *exits. Pause. He enters.*)

ELLIS: Yes, she's gone.

JOANNA: The poor woman.

ELLIS: There's nothing we could do.

JOANNA: What's going on out there, Ellis?

ELLIS: I told you, didn't I? They're all at it.
  (*Pause.*)

JOANNA: Dear God. Why?

BLACKOUT

54521